D0947652

GLEN HANSON and ALLAN NEUWIRTH

 alyson books
los angeles

ALL CHARACTERS IN THIS BOOK ARE FICTITIOUS. ANY RESEMBLANCE TO REAL INDIVIDUALS—EITHER LIVING OR DEAD—IS STRICTLY COINCIDENTAL.

© 2003 BY GLEN HANSON AND ALLAN NEUWIRTH. ALL RIGHTS RESERVED.

MANUFACTURED IN CANADA.

THIS TRADE PAPERBACK ORIGINAL IS PUBLISHED BY ALYSON PUBLICATIONS,
P.O. BOX 4371, LOS ANGELES, CALIFORNIA 90078-4371.
DISTRIBUTION IN THE UNITED KINGDOM BY TURNAROUND PUBLISHER SERVICES LTD.,
UNIT 3, OLYMPIA TRADING ESTATE, COBURG ROAD, WOOD GREEN,
LONDON N22 6TZ ENGLAND.

FIRST EDITION: SEPTEMBER 2003

03 04 05 06 07 a 10 9 8 7 6 5 4 3 2 1

ISBN 1-55583-820-0

LIBRARY OF CONGRESS CATALOGING-IN-PUBLICATION DATA
HANSON, GLEN.
  CHELSEA BOYS / GLEN HANSON AND ALLAN NEUWIRTH.—1ST ED.
  ISBN 1-55583-820-0
  I. NEUWIRTH, ALLAN. II. TITLE.
PN6728.C54H36 2003
741.5'973.—DC21   2003052219

FOREWORD

Howard Cruse

I was once a Chelsea boy—but that was quite a while back, in 1969, and it didn't last long. I was a 25-year-old Alabama refugee trying and largely failing to draw cartoons that New York art directors would find amusing.

My tiny apartment on 15th Street near 8th Avenue was roughly the size and shape of a hallway. There were no closets in it, unless you count the one inside my head that convinced me I could never allow my homosexuality to be discernible in my published comics if I wanted to have a "real" cartooning career. There was room in my apartment for me to walk back and forth while lost in thought—a core requirement for an artistic dreamer—but only if I included the bathroom in my pacing path. It was clearly not designed for multiple occupancy.

So I have no stories to tell about fascinating roommates like hunky Sky and sublime Soirée, the archetypes that shlubby everygayman Nathan gathers into his nest in Glen Hanson and Allan Neuwirth's comic strip "Chelsea Boys." This is just as well, since I might have been tempted to incorporate such interesting free spirits into my own comics, and that way lay disaster. Happily, times have changed for lesbian and gay cartoonists. The Stonewall riots erupted a few blocks downtown from me that summer, and Gay Power handbills began appearing everywhere in the days that followed. From the first, fresh winds seemed to be blowing, but I underestimated by far the degree of change those riots portended for all of us—even us lowly comic strip creators.

In 1969 the queer center of gravity hadn't yet shifted upward from Greenwich Village. That transpired later. So my personal associations with being young and gay in Chelsea don't include the buff, campy, and sexually overheated queer sidewalk scene that serves as the "Chelsea Boys" backdrop. I recognize the Chelsea that Neuwirth and Hanson are depicting, however. Although my lover and I set up housekeeping 24 years ago across the East River in Jackson Heights, life takes me to Chelsea from time to time, and my jaw often drops at the sculpted male bodies strolling there. Chelsea, being a diverse neighborhood with a rich history, isn't totally defined by the gym gods who make me feel both invigorated and elderly, but they certainly dress it up well.

Glen Hanson is a perfect cartoonist to depict Chelsea's gay scene. Glen is an excellent caricaturist, and I've never known a gay-centric environment that didn't serve up plenty of fair targets for caricature. While most gays are visually unidentifiable, not all are, and wherever the freedom to be over-the-top without penalty exists, people temperamentally inclined toward over-the-topness will step forward to mine that freedom. The Soirées of the world will take to whatever stages are available (and don't think that a line at the local deli's salad bar won't suffice), and the Skys of the world will amplify a cityscape's beauty by going shirtless. Hanson's observant eye has much to work with in this neighborhood, and nothing draws a good cartoonist like people who are fun to draw.

Writer Allan Neuwirth and Hanson, as longstanding and comfortable collaborators, work together to chart and script the feature's story lines, filling the strip's word balloons with dialogue that nudges the characters past and beyond the pitfalls of stereotypes. I salute them for crafting dialogue that is insightful, not just setups for gags. They strive for nuance, which means that obviousness is nudged aside in favor of unpredictability.

True to its title, "Chelsea Boys" comes dressed in Chelsea-isms. Its characters' yearnings and insecurities, however, are not geography-specific. As rooted in time-and-place specifics as "Chelsea Boys" can be—when terrorists strike on September 11, the strip stops to shudder along with the rest of New York City—the more commonplace plot turns, like Sky's fumbles in forging a partnership, Nathan's adventure in procreation, and Soirée's bid for a dying father's approval, don't need Manhattan landmarks in order to resonate.

"Chelsea Boys" may be a comic strip about the trials and tribulations of three Big Apple roommates, but you won't mistake it for "Apartment 3-G." Worlds of traffic-filled blocks lie between the latter strip's hetero-heartbreak glamour and the down-to-earth doings in Nathan's digs. Comedy is the currency in play here, but it is comedy with heart. Watch the story expand its reach beyond standard gay fare as you turn the pages of this compilation. Watch the characters reveal the intriguing parts of themselves that play against first impressions. Watch yourself get caught up in the flow and find more of your life reflected in "Chelsea Boys" than you may have expected—even those of you who live miles and cultures away from Hanson and Neuwirth's title locale.

INTRODUCTION

"Chelsea Boys"...The Early Days

Before you start chuckling at the cartoons, we thought it might be fun to give you a peek at "Chelsea Boys"' humble beginnings, in the hopes that you may better appreciate all the rich, home-baked goodness of the comic strips themselves. Yeah, we know you didn't plunk down your 14 bucks to read the semicoherent musings of a pair of cartoon-creatin' fags. You thought you were purchasing an anthology of the finest gay comics your money could buy, didn't you? Well, the joke's on you. (Then again, if you just skip over this intro, the joke's on us.)

The comic strip actually began as something else. Since animation is a big part of our careers, our original intent was to create a gay-themed animated cartoon short called *Think Pink.* So we assembled a small army of creative folk and began brainstorming and writing...before we realized there were too many different opinions—and just too many cooks in the kitchen.

It all started when one of us, while still living up north in that freezing wonderland known as Canada (Glen, that crazy Canuck), started dreaming up characters for an animated series centered around three gay roommates. (This was 1994, before *Ellen, Will & Grace*, or *Queer As Folk.* Boy, we've come a long way!) They first sprang to life as three archetypal queer icons: a tough little leather daddy; a flamboyant, gender-bending performance diva; and a muscled artist who works as a go-go boy. As you can see from the early sketches, they weren't *too* far off physically from the characters they eventually became. Their personalities, however, changed dramatically.

Once we began collaborating on the 'toon—just the two of us, that is—we realized that the last thing either of us wanted to do was depict the adventures of three stereotypes. People are rarely who we think they are at first glance, and we wanted our project to reflect that. We wanted characters with dimension that people could relate to.

Nathan underwent the most dramatic persona adjustment as we began to create a central character that we—as well as our audience—might be able to better identify with. And so, instead of

[The very first incarnation of Nathan, whom we were going to call Vince]

being a hot, aggressive little V-shaped leather dude, Nathan became more of a dumpy, insecure, pear-shaped everyman...sort of a gay Charlie Brown who—like most of us—just longs for a loving relationship. This enabled us to more easily use Nathan as a surrogate mouthpiece for many of our opinions and observations (even though neither of us is pint-size or dumpy). He also morphed from Italian to Jewish and acquired a last name along the way: Klein.

Soirée changed the least. Since he was angular, glam, and ultra-fabulous from the get-go, we merely had to flesh out his complex personality, give him a rich and turbulent back story, and determine how he'd mesh with the others. His birth name began on paper as Sylvester Munroe and finally ended up Delroy Monroe.

[Soirée dripped attitude and feline grace, even in these early sketches.]

The strip's most popular character, Sky (at first named Ethan), also underwent some alterations as we developed our little opus. In our original treatment we described him thusly:

"A bright 22-year-old tortured artist trapped in the body of a god. Ethan could have the world at his feet but makes life impossible for himself

by being different. He longs to be taken seriously, but because he won the genetic lottery he's rarely looked at as anything more than a sex object; this makes him more than a bit cynical. He came to New York to attend art school and works part time as a go-go boy at the hottest Chelsea dance club, Olympus."

Sky was initially conceived as a massively muscled Chelsea boy clone with a tiny Jack Russell terrier. But his facial features softened (even if his body didn't) and he became more of an innocent—transplanted to NYC from a Canadian farming collective: creative, spiritual, and idealistic, the child of former hippies–1960s peace activists (whom we later named Sun and Moon). Suddenly the name Sky sounded more appropriate for this character. (Our little inside joke was that drop-dead gorgeous Sky is, in fact, the *runt* of the litter; his siblings—Storm, Forest, Meadow, and Sunflower—are far more beautiful than he is.)

[Check out Ethan/Sky's huge cleft chin...which we felt made him look a bit too tough.]

Sky's little dog, Capote, became Nathan's instead—renamed Miss Marmelstein after Barbra Streisand's character in her first big hit, the Broadway show "I Can Get It for You Wholesale." Perky Miss M. turned into Nathan's constant and most loyal companion, butting heads with the catlike Soirée and adoring the animal-loving Sky.

As we pressed on with our efforts to launch *Think Pink,* we were advised to create public awareness for our characters in print first...so we decided to kick off with a syndicated cartoon strip. But what to call it? We bounced many potential names back and forth, then finally settled on a spin on Andy

[Though she began as a he, named after Truman Capote, Miss M's design stayed the same.]

Warhol's famous underground film *The Chelsea Girls*: We christened our child "Chelsea Boys."

Since we had contacts at *Next* magazine in New York City, it made sense for us to start there...and so we did: "Chelsea Boys" began running as a comic strip in August 1998. Weekly.

Which nearly killed us. In our naïveté, it never occurred to us how much *work* a syndicated strip entailed. It turned out that conceiving, writing, sketching, revising, penciling, inking, scanning, cleaning up, and disseminating a new installment every week—on top of our hectic freelance work schedules—proved just about impossible.

So "Chelsea Boys" quickly became a biweekly strip...and even that turned out to be a formidable task. Through most of the strip's five years, we've worked individually (and sometimes in collaboration) on all of our other respective projects—including writing, designing, art directing, and producing cartoon TV series for network and cable, illustrating and writing books, designing ads and CD covers, writing and/or illustrating comic books and graphic novels, and on and on...while continuing to create and distribute "Chelsea Boys" at the same time.

All this remains a delicate balancing act. Some of the commercial jobs we take on may not nurture our souls the way creating "Chelsea Boys" does, but they pay the bills and put food on the table. Hey, Papa's still gotta eat. (And not just dick.)

Even though the end result has been unbelievably gratifying, we can't recommend our schedules to anyone who desires a

semblance of a normal life. We often liken the strip to a very young baby: No matter what else you're doing at the time, when the baby starts to cry, you have to run to it and take care of it. Come hell or high water, we have to turn out a new comic strip every other week.

As the readership of "Chelsea Boys" has grown—the comic now appears in dozens of publications and Web sites across the U.S., Canada, and the U.K.—our concerns have shifted. In the beginning we worried more about gags and visuals—so if you look at the first group of strips, you'll note how joke-oriented they are and how cohesively each page is designed. Over time we realized that it's truly more about the storytelling—not that we ignored the pretty visuals or the laughs, they just didn't seem *as* important—so that became our emphasis. As you read through the first 100 installments, you'll hopefully see how the strip evolved year by year; how the tone of "Chelsea Boys" started out much lighter and more satiric but eventually became more character- and story-driven.

In the course of putting this book—our very first bound collection—together, we had to go through all the material again. It was interesting how so many memories came rushing back at us, brought on by specific strips and story lines. Some of them reflected events going on in our lives, or our friends' lives, at the time. Others mirrored the political climate of the world, or simply where we were emotionally when we wrote and created them—depressed, elated, over-worked, in love, fearful, or just eager to talk. To this end, we consider ourselves lucky to have a forum in which to express ourselves, and grateful as hell that so many readers identify with our thoughts and concerns.

Over the years we've been asked many questions by our readers. So here's our opportunity to answer the ones we've been asked most often.

Who draws the strip and who writes it?

"Chelsea Boys" is a completely collaborative creative endeavor. Since we can both write and draw, we conceive and script each installment together—often acting them out—before one of us (Glen) sits down to illustrate. We then review the rough sketch together to make changes in the dialogue and visuals, before the pencils are cleaned up (again by Glen) and inked (usually by Angelo Divino) and then cleaned up again (by Allan) on computer. On very rare occasions, the *other* one of us (Allan) will assemble or illustrate a strip—such as the installment on page 100, designed to look like it was drawn by Nathan's young nephew, Jason.

Who are the characters modeled on? Are they really you?

The fact is, we're none of them—and all of them—at once. The characters spring from our imaginations, and are equal parts *us* and friends/acquaintances. Sometimes someone we know will say something that might inspire a story, but we never just plunk our friends into the "Chelsea Boys" world. Occasionally we lampoon a famous personality or two (these will be obvious as you read the strips). When Nathan and his best friend, Richard, get into philosophical or political discussions, they reflect our own conversations, to a degree...with Nathan's opinions often closest to our own.

Are you two guys, ya know, like "partners"?

No, we're not romantically involved. We're best friends and collaborators who love working together. (We actually met through the *Think Pink* project, when Glen was searching for a gay animation producer for the original TV show idea!)

With such a hectic work schedule, how do you both manage to stay looking so fabulous?

You're too kind, really.

OK. So now you've read paragraph after paragraph about us...and lest you think that we've done this all by ourselves, here are some people who've helped us out along the way:

A big thank you goes out to Angelo Divino, who began inking most of the strips starting in 2000 and has done a wonderful job right on through to the present day. Special thanks also go

[A typical "Chelsea Boys" pencil rough, drawn by Glen, before we dive in to make our revisions]

["Chelsea Boys" creators, Glen and Allan. We do look fabulous, and kinda cartoony, don't we?]

to the artist Dino Alberto, who inked a few early installments, and to Jim Arnoff, Charles Busch, Alan Cumming, Chris Davis, Frank DeCaro, Angelo DeCesare, Marc Easton, Ariel Estrada, Karyn Hanson Schmidt, Ron Kanfi, Ken Katsumoto, Kim Kondracki, Mark Lieber, Lou Maletta, Rodger McFarlane, Michael Musto, Risa Neuwirth, John Olson, Kurt Pacquette, Jason Reilley, Marty Rotman, Nelson Sarmiento, Alan Scott, Linda Simensky, Albert Simic, Daniel Springer, Bruce Vilanch, Andrew Volkoff, and our good friend Peter Winter, who all generously offered us inspiration, support, advice, and/or blurbs for our book jacket; to Mike Caffey, Sam Tallerico, and Mark Watrel, for their early participation in the *Think Pink* short; to Howard Cruse, who not only laid the groundwork for openly gay comix with his wonderfully perceptive strip *Wendel* and brilliant graphic novel *Stuck Rubber Baby* but also graciously agreed to pen the foreword to this collection; to Sidney Clifton and Peter Schankowitz at Film Roman; to Angela Brown, Terri Fabris, and Matt Sams at Alyson Books; and to Mark Kondracki, our talented Webmaster and "Chelsea Boys" Web site designer, who expanded our world and helped launch us into the modern cyber age.

Last but not least, we'd like to thank all the editors, publishers, and staff of the many publications who've run us over the years and continue to carry our strip...but most important, our readers—who've shared their ideas, comments, praise, and even criticism with us, and let us know that they've been amused and touched and inspired by our work. For us, that's the greatest reward of all.

ALLAN NEUWIRTH
and
GLEN HANSON

© 1998 HANSON and NEUWIRTH

(16)

(17)

CHELSEA BOYS

BY GLEN HANSON and ALLAN NEUWIRTH

NATHAN, OUT WALKING ALONG THE PIER WITH HIS BEST FRIEND RICHARD, WALLOWS IN MISERY...

GOD-- HOW **STUPID** WAS I, TAKING IN A ROOMMATE I HAD THE HOTS FOR? AS IF **SKY** WAS GONNA FALL FOR **ME**, THE SHORT DUMPY GUY WITH THE HAIRY BACK... WHAT WAS I **THINKING**?

YOU WEREN'T THINKING NATHAN. **MR. PEE-PEE** WAS DOING THE THINKING FOR YOU.

≥SIGH≤ WHY DON'T I JUST GIVE UP? I HAD PAUL, AND NOW HE'S GONE... LET'S FACE IT, I'M GONNA BE ALONE FOR THE REST OF MY LIFE...

HONEY, **PUH-LEEZE.** YOU HAVE **GOT** TO STOP FEELING SORRY FOR YOURSELF!

THAT'S EASY FOR YOU TO SAY -- YOU HAVE **RUBEN.**

UH-HUH! AND Y'KNOW WHERE WE MET? THE **LAUNDROMAT!** ≥ HA HA ≤ WE GOT OUR UNDERWEAR MIXED UP...

THAT KEPT HAPPENING, EVEN AFTER WE MOVED IN TOGETHER... SO NOW, WE JUST DON'T WEAR ANY!

THANK YOU, RICHARD. THAT'S MORE INFORMATION THAN I NEEDED TO KNOW.

THE POINT IS, YA NEVER KNOW WHEN OR WHERE YOU'RE GONNA MEET SOMEONE. IN FACT... DON'T LOOK NOW, BUT I THINK THAT CUTIE OVER THERE IS CRUISING YOU!

OH, **GET REAL!!** GUYS WHO LOOK LIKE **THAT** DON'T CRUISE GUYS WHO LOOK LIKE **ME!!**

GOD, LOOK AT THAT GUY OVER THERE... SHORT, DARK, AND CUTE -- JUST MY TYPE... AND OF COURSE HE'S GOT A BOYFRIEND! ≥SIGH≤

© 1998 HANSON AND NEUWIRTH

(24)

[Early pencil-and-marker characer designs of the boys, by Glen Hanson.]

© 2002 HANSON + NEUWIRTH

CHELSEABOYS.COM

(29)

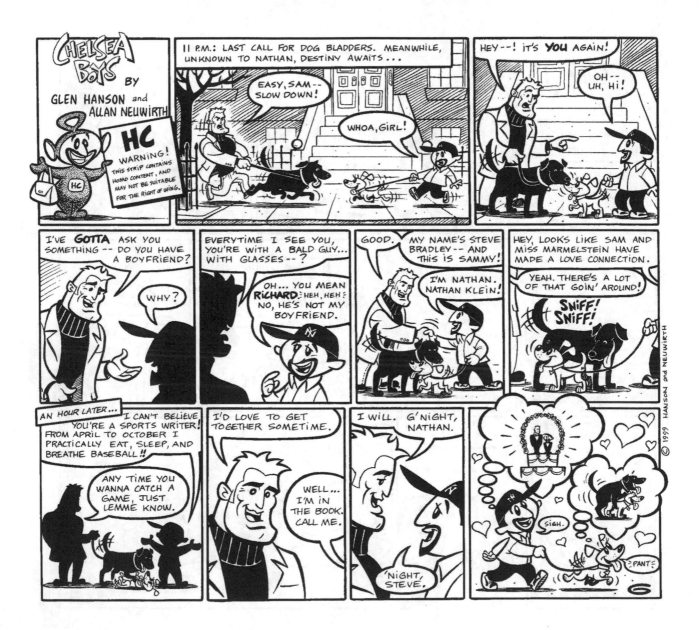

(36)

© 1999 HANSON + NEUWIRTH

WWW.CHELSEABOYS.COM

(40)

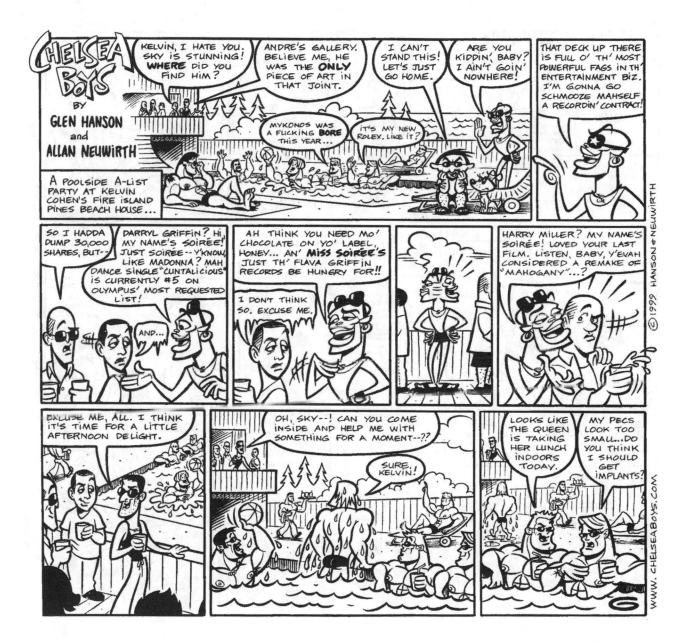

(46)

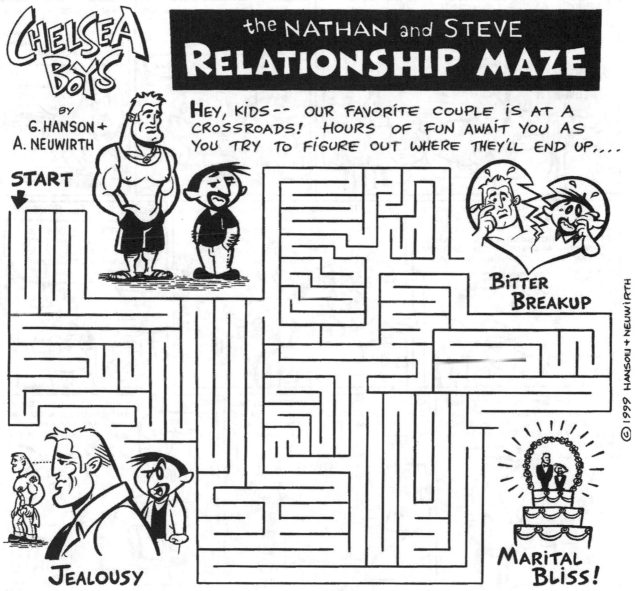

(53)

CHELSEA BOYS

BY GLEN HANSON and ALLAN NEUWIRTH

NATHAN MAKES A BREAKTHROUGH AT HIS WEEKLY BARBRAHOLICS ANONYMOUS MEETING...

SO LAST WEEK I BROKE UP WITH MY BOYFRIEND AND MY FIRST IMPULSE WAS THE OL' YENTL AND HÄAGEN-DAZS. BUT I CALLED COREY, AND HE HELPED ME REALIZE THAT I CAN GET THROUGH A CRISIS ON MY OWN.

ANONYMOUS

PUT THE MEMORIES BEHIND YOU!

SEE, GUYS? YOU **DON'T** HAVE TO BE THE WAY YOU WERE! AND NOW, NATHAN, IT'S TIME TO TAKE THE FINAL STEP TO FREEDOM, AND SURRENDER ALL YOUR BARBRAPHERNALIA!

83 MINUTES LATER...

...AND FINALLY MY MOST CHERISHED POSSESSION: A BAGEL BARBRA TOOK A BITE OUT OF DURING THE ORIGINAL RUN OF "FUNNY GIRL" IN 1964.

OOOH AHHHH

PEOP

BARBRAHOLI NONYMOUS

CLAP!

CHEER! CLAP!

AFTER...

I HAVE TO ADMIT, NATHAN, WHEN I SAW THAT MOLDY OLD BAGEL -- I WANTED IT BAD...

SO BADLY THAT I WOULD HAVE FUCKED **JESSE HELMS** ALL NIGHT LONG TO GET IT.!!

HI MY NAME IS FRANCINE

BUT THAT WAS THE OLD ME. NOW, I HAVE **NO PROBLEM** THAT COREY JUST TOSSED ALL THAT IRREPLACEABLE BARBRAPHERNALIA IN THE DUMPSTER OUT BACK...

'SCUSE ME FOR A MOMENT, WON'T YOU--?

I'M SO PROUD OF YOU, NATHAN!

≶URMF≶ THANKS... LAWRENCE-- ≶UNHH≶

SQUEEZE!

WHAT YOU DID WAS **SO** AMAZING... I JUST CAN'T BRING MYSELF TO LET GO YET.

WELL... HOPEFULLY SOMEDAY YOU WILL... GOD WILLING...

I DON'T KNOW WHAT IT IS ABOUT YOU, NATHAN, BUT I JUST **HAVE** TO GIVE YOU **ANOTHER HUG!!**

CHELSEA BOYS

BY **GLEN HANSON** and **ALLAN NEUWIRTH**

SUNDAY IN THE PARK WITH **NATHAN**, HIS SISTER **RISA**, AND HER TWO BOYS...

--SO THERE WE WERE, STANDING IN MY DOORWAY AT ONE A.M.: ME, THIS HUSTLER...AND MOM, HANDING ME A POT OF MEATBALLS!

HA HA HA OMIGOD-- THAT'S HILARIOUS!! NOT EXACTLY THE MEAT OR BALLS YOU HAD IN MIND, HUH...

I MEAN, YA GOTTA ADMIT-- THAT'S **WEIRD**, EVEN FOR MOM...

YEAH...LAST WEEK SHE CALLED ME 5 TIMES IN A ROW TO ASK WHAT DAY IT WAS. I'M ACTUALLY STARTING TO WORRY ABOUT HER.

OWW!

MOMMY! JUSTIN HIT ME WITH THE BALL!

SHUT UP, WIENER-FACE!! I DID NOT!

GAP

JUSTIN, JASON-- WHAT DID I TELL YOU ABOUT FIGHTING?!!

UGH...THOSE TWO KIDS ARE GONNA DRIVE ME NUTS...

BOY, I DON'T KNOW HOW YOU DO IT. **I** COULDN'T... I THINK I'M GONNA SAY NO TO RICKI AND LUCIE...

NO, NATHAN -- I'VE BEEN THINKING ABOUT THAT... YOU'D MAKE A **GREAT** FATHER! JUSTIN AND JASON BOTH LOVE YOU!

I DUNNO, REESE...

THEY JUST ASKED FOR MY SPERM, Y'KNOW... EVEN IF THEY **DID** WANT ME TO STICK AROUND AND BE THE BABY'S FATHER, I'M NOT SURE IF I'M CUT OUT TO BE A PARENT.

NATHAN, EVERYONE HAS DOUBTS AND FEARS ABOUT THAT.

RAISING MY KIDS HAS BEEN THE MOST CHALLENGING, MAGICAL, FULFILLING EXPERIENCE OF MY LIFE. I WOULDN'T TRADE IT FOR ANYTHING!

BONK!

IF YOU TWO DON'T CUT IT OUT I'M GONNA THROTTLE YOU!!

© 2000 HANSON + NEUWIRTH

CHELSEABOYS.COM

(64)

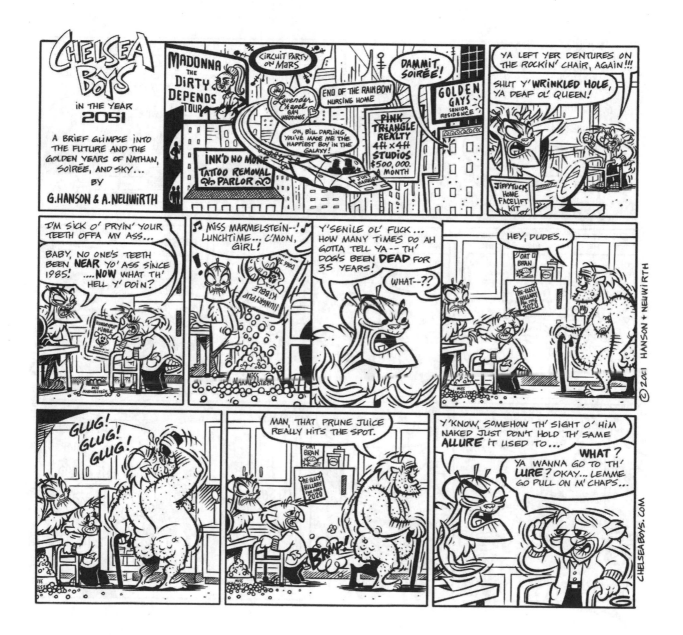

CHELSEA BOYS

BY G. HANSON and A. NEUWIRTH

SOMEWHERE IN MIDTOWN, NATHAN AND RICHARD HAIL A CAB...

I STILL CAN'T BELIEVE IT... ONE MINUTE STEVE WAS SITTING AT HIS DESK, WORKING... AND NOW HE'S GONE--FOREVER...

22ND AND NINTH, PLEASE.

HONK

GOD... I KNOW THINGS DIDN'T END WELL BETWEEN US... BUT NOW I WISH I COULD'VE SPOKEN TO HIM ONE LAST TIME-- OR TOLD HIM THAT I CARED ABOUT HIM.

I **HATE** THAT BASTARD BIN LADEN AND THOSE FUCKERS FOR WHAT THEY'VE DONE--

I'D BE HAPPY TO GO OVER THERE **MYSELF** RIGHT NOW AND **BOMB THE SHIT** OUT OF ALL OF 'EM!

RICHARD, ARE YOU KIDDING ME? WHAT'S **THAT** GONNA SOLVE -- OTHER THAN KILLING THOUSANDS OF INNOCENT PEOPLE?! BOMBING AFGHANISTAN ISN'T GONNA PUT AN END TO **TERRORISM**.

WE'RE AT **WAR**, NATHAN! YOU CAN'T HAVE A WAR WITHOUT LOSING SOME INNOCENT LIVES. WHAT WERE WE SUPPOSED TO DO-- JUST TAKE IT AND DO **NOTHING** ??

OF COURSE NOT. I JUST DON'T THINK WE SHOULD BLINDLY REACT OUT OF ANGER... WE NEED TO GATHER INFORMATION NOW, WE NEED TO --

WHATEVER, I STILL SAY **BOMB THEIR ASSES!** MAYBE THAT'LL MAKE THEM THINK TWICE BEFORE THEY--

EXCUSE ME, MY FRIEND...

BEFORE YOU GO DROPPING YOUR BOMBS -- I STILL HAVE TWO BROTHERS AND A MOTHER AND FATHER LIVING IN KABUL. THEY HAD NOTHING TO DO WITH WHAT HAPPENED.

WHY DO YOU THINK I HAVE ALL THESE FLAGS DECORATING MY TAXICAB? TO SHOW EVERY ONE THAT EVEN THOUGH I'VE HAD MY **LIFE THREATENED** AND MY CHILDREN HAVE BEEN **SPAT ON**-- AND YES, I AM **AFRAID**--THAT I'M AN AMERICAN, TOO...

HERE WE ARE. THAT'S $6.20

PLEASE, KEEP THE CHANGE. AND DON'T WORRY ABOUT MY FRIEND HERE. YOU'LL NEVER CATCH HIM IN CAMOUFLAGE --UNLESS THEY START SELLING IT AT **ARMANI**.

© 2001 HANSON + NEUWIRTH

CHELSEABOYS.COM

(82)

(84)

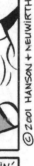

CHELSEA BOYS

BY
GLEN HANSON
and
ALLAN NEUWIRTH

NATHAN VISITS HIS SISTER RISA AND HER FAMILY FOR DINNER...

THAT WAS A GREAT MEAL, REESE. YOU ARE THE **BEST** COOK.

THANKS, NATE. HERE YA GO...

THANKS.

SO WHAT'S UP WITH DAVE? SEEMED LIKE HE WAS IN A REALLY WEIRD MOOD AT DINNER.

OH, HE'S JUST IN A SNIT LATELY CAUSE EVERYONE KEEPS TELLING US THEY THINK JASON'S GONNA GROW UP TO BE **GAY**.

WHADDAYA MEAN? DAVE'S ALWAYS BEEN COOL WITH **ME**-- BESIDES, THE KID'S JUST SIX YEARS OLD. HOW CAN ANYONE TELL IF HE'S GONNA BE GAY??

NATHAN. SEE THIS PRETTY BRACELET I'M WEARING? Y'KNOW WHO MADE IT FOR ME? MY **SON**.

THE SAME KID WHO LOVES BARBIE DOLLS... AND WANTS TO DO MY HAIR ALL THE TIME... AND PICKS OUT MY CLOTHES FOR ME BEFORE I GO TO WORK.

SO WHAT? THAT'S **SO** CLICHÉ... THE KID JUST HAS A GOOD FASHION SENSE.

MOMMY...

IF I GO GET THE POLISH, CAN WE PAINT OUR NAILS TOGETHER?

SURE, MUNCHKIN.

YOU KNOW WHERE IT IS-- RIGHT ON MY DRESSER.

YAY!!

HMMM... MAYBE YOU'RE RIGHT...

WHATEVER. I'M NOT WORRIED ABOUT JASON. EITHER WAY, HE'LL BE JUST FINE.

BESIDES, THE KID'S SCHMECKEL IS ALREADY BIGGER THAN HIS DAD'S. HE'S GONNA BE **REAL POPULAR**!

≷GIGGLE≷

© 2002 HANSON + NEUWIRTH

CHELSEABOYS.COM

(93)

CHELSEA BOYS

BY GLEN HANSON and ALLAN NEUWIRTH

Soirée's sister Karen arrives at his apartment for a midday lunch date...

BZZZ BZZZ

UH, HI -- IS DELROY HERE?

OH, IS THAT HIS NAME? YEAH, WHATEVER...

HEY, BABY SISTER.

DELROY--! WHO WAS **THAT**?

OH, JUST A HOOKUP.

A "HOOKUP"? IN THE MIDDLE OF THE DAY? BRO, WHEN YOU GONNA FIND YOURSELF A **REAL** BOYFRIEND AND SETTLE DOWN?

WHEN ANTONIO BANDERAS ASKS ME T'MARRY HIM.

WELL, HERE'S THE MONEY YOU NEEDED... I'M SORRY IT ISN'T MORE. THEY DON'T PAY INTERNS THAT MUCH, THEY JUST **WORK** US TO DEATH!

THANKS, KAREN. THIS'LL REALLY HELP ME OUT... IT'S BEEN HARD T'FIND A JOB.

HMMM. IT MIGHT BE EASIER TO FIND A JOB IF YOU SPENT THE DAYS **LOOKING** FOR ONE INSTEAD OF WASTING YOUR TIME HOOKING UP.

'SCUSE ME, BUT WHAT I DO WITH MAH TIME AIN'T REALLY NONE O' YOUR BUSINESS.

YOU **ARE** MY BUSINESS, CUZ YOU'RE MY BROTHER AND I CARE ABOUT YOU. BESIDES, YOU SAID YOU WERE BUSTING YOUR A$$ TRYING TO GET WORK-- AND THAT'S NOT WHAT I'M SEEING.

© 2002 HANSON AND NEUWIRTH

YEAH? YOU GIVIN' ME THIS MONEY DOESN'T GIVE YOU THE RIGHT TO TELL ME HOW TO LIVE.

WELL, **SOMEONE** SURE NEEDS TO SET YOU STRAIGHT.

IF THAT'S THE WAY YOU FEEL, KEEP YO' DAMN MONEY, BITCH! I DON'T NEED IT!

FINE! THEN I WILL! YOU CAN JUST GET BY ON YOUR OWN!

SLAM!!

FUCK THAT SHIT!

MOMENTS LATER...

lick your feet, Sir. your knees, boy! es, Sir...

Respond

Instant Message

BlkTop4you: Hey, boy... u sound like you're damn hungry for it. Home alone here and horned... wanna come over?

Respond | Cancel | Get Profile | Notify Us

CHELSEABOYS.COM

(95)

CHELSEA BOYS

by
Glen Hanson
&
Allan Neuwirth

There were once two hot young boys who loved each other very much.

One day when they were apart, one of them followed his dick instead of his head.

But he was a little pussy, and he couldn't tell the other boy about it...

Unfortunately, both boys were in for a *big* surprise.

GONORRHEA

This didn't help their relationship at all.

SLAP!

The first boy was very sad, and he moped around with a long boo-boo face for a whole week.

He called...

~CLICK~

HELLO?

BLOCKED

And he wrote...

And he begged.

And finally...

They talked, and they talked, and they talked...

...until the second boy forgave him, but warned him if he ever did anything like that again, he'd kick his bitch ass to the curb.

They were both so happy, they got all horned up and wanted to have hot make-up sex...

...but they both still had an STD. So they took their medication and just cuddled.

The End.

© 2002 HANSON+NEUWIRTH

CHELSEABOYS.COM

CHELSEA BOYS

MY WEEKEND WITH UNCLE NATHAN, UNCLE SKY, and ~~AUNT~~ UNCLE SOIRÉE (AND MISS MARMULSTEEN)

BY JASON HARRIS

ON FRIDAY WE WENT TO SEE "SUGAR PONY'S MAGIC ADVENTURE." IT WAS GREAT.

Me

Z Z Z Z Z

POP CORN

UNCLE NATHAN

Food →

LATER WE WENT TO McDONALD'S. YUM!

UNCLE SKY TOOK ME FOR ICE CREAM. EVERYONE WAS REALLY REALLY FRIENDLY.

HEY SEXY DADDY

whistle

I MET TWO MOMMIES NAMED RICKY + LUCIE + THEIR BABY LINDSAY. THEY THINK SHE IS SO CUTE...

UNCLE SOIRÉE SAYS THE BABY LOOKS LIKE SHE CAME FROM THE UGLY FARM. HA HA!

← BABY

WE TOOK MISS M. FOR A WALK. IT WAS FUN EXCEPT WE HAD TO PICK UP HER POO.

P.U.

ON SUNDAY I PLAYED FASHION SHOW WITH UNCLE SOIRÉE...

CLAP
CLAP
CLAP
CLAP!
CLAP

HOME AGAIN !!!

"I CAN'T WAIT TO VISIT MY UNCLES AGAIN EVEN THOUGH DADDY SAYS THEY'RE A BAD FLUENCE ON ME.

HEY SEXY DADDY

© 2002 HANSON + NEUWIRTH

CHELSEABOYS.COM

(100)

CHELSEA BOYS

BY

HANSON & NEUWIRTH

Arriving for a simple hook-up, Soirée is confronted by something he never expected...

I DIDN'T COME HERE FO' THIS SHIT. IF WE AIN'T GONNA FUCK, I'M GONE.

WAIT A MINUTE -- I WAS SERIOUS. I REALLY DO WANNA KNOW WHO YOU ARE.

YOU WANNA KNOW WHO I AM? YEAH. OKAY. EVER HEARD OF SOIRÉE?

Y'MEAN THE CLUB DRAG DIVA? THAT'S YOU?

YEAH. TH' QUEEN WHO WEARS MAKEUP AND HEELS AND FEATHERS AND SHIT, STRUTTIN' AROUN' ON STAGE AND SHAKIN' HER ASS? WOULD YOU STILL HAVE WANTED ME T' FUCK YOU IF YOU KNEW WHO I WAS?

WELL, MAYBE...

I'D RATHER BE WITH THE **REAL YOU** THAN SOME ARTIFICIAL TOP MAN RECITIN' DIALOGUE YOU THINK I'LL FIND HOT... LOOKIN' IN YOUR EYES RIGHT NOW, I'M GETTIN' THAT THERE'S WAY MORE TO YOU THAN THAT.

I MEAN, IT'S NOT HARD TO SEE THAT YOU'VE GOT A LOT OF ANGER... BUT I CAN ALSO SEE YOUR SENSITIVITY.

WHAT'RE YOU, A SHRINK?

NO. JUST A BROTHER WHO SEES ANOTHER BROTHER THAT'S DOIN' EVERYTHING HE CAN TO HIDE WHO HE REALLY IS.

SO WHAT D'YOU WANT FROM ME?

WELL, ⸢CHUCKLE⸣ I **WAS** EXPECTING TO GET LAID TONIGHT... BUT IF YOU WANNA SIT ON THE COUCH AND JUST TALK, THAT'S COOL WITH ME.

LATER...

YEAH, CURTIS... BUT LOOK AT YOU. BIG CORPORATE LAWYER... A TIGHT CRIB... ALL THIS ART... A HOUSE IN THE PINES... WHAT DO I GOT? I'M AN OUTTA WORK PATTERNMAKER AN' A WASHED UP DRAG QUEEN.

HEY, DON'T BEAT YOURSELF UP, DELROY. I WORKED **DAMN HARD** FOR A LOT OF YEARS. I STRUGGLED... MADE A LOT OF SACRIFICES. IT WASN'T EASY, BUT NOTHING WORTHWHILE HAPPENS OVERNIGHT. YOU CAN'T GIVE UP.

FUCK THAT SHIT... Y'KNOW HOW HARD I'VE WORKED TH' PAST TEN YEARS? WHAT I'VE GONE THROUGH?! ALWAYS HAVIN' T' BE "ON"... ALWAYS HAVIN' T' BE "FABULOUS"... AN' JUST WHEN EVERYTHING WAS **THIS CLOSE** T' HAPPENING, IT ALL FELL APART!

I JUS' CAN'T DO IT ANYMORE... I JUST... I --

© 2002 HANSON + NEUWIRTH

CHELSEABOYS.COM

CHELSEA BOYS

BY

HANSON AND NEUWIRTH

WAR

WHAT DO YOU THINK?

LOOK, I'M A LIBERAL FROM WAY BACK. AND I THINK BUSH IS A **MORON**... BUT I'M TORN. I **HATE** WAR, BUT SHOULD WE JUST SIT AROUND WAITING FOR THESE LUNATICS TO BLOW US UP?

THIS IS ALL BECAUSE OF **MEN**, WITH THEIR FUCKING OVERLOAD OF TESTOSTERONE AND THEIR POWER-MAD DELUSIONS. IT'S A CONTEST TO SEE WHOSE DICK IS BIGGER. THESE GUYS WON'T BE SATISFIED TILL THE WORLD IS **DECIMATED**.

WHATEVER. WHO AM I TO CRITICIZE OUR PRESIDENT? ALL I KNOW IS THE **BUSH TWINS** WERE AT MY LAST SHOW AND THEY EACH BOUGHT **TEN PIECES** RIGHT OFF THE RUNWAY! THEY'RE **FABULOUS**!

PEOPLE ARE, LIKE, MISSING THE POINT OF LIFE. IT'S ALL ABOUT **LOVE**. IF EVERYONE WOULD JUST SLOW DOWN, MEDITATE, AND LOOK INSIDE THEMSELVES, THEY'D SEE THE TRUTH.

C'MON! THIS IS ABOUT **MONEY**. WAR IS BIG BUSINESS -- BUSH AND HIS WHOLE REPUBLICAN CABINET, THEY'RE ALL **BIG OIL**. WE'RE FIGHTIN' FOR THE MONEY OF THE **FEW**.

BABY, I THINK **MISS DUBYA** AN' **SADDAM INSANE** BOTH JUS' NEED A **GOOD COCKTAIL** AN' A **BIG DICK** UP THEIR ASS.

YOU KNOW WHO'S **REALLY** GONNA SUFFER IN THIS WAR? IT WON'T BE THE RELATIVES OR FAMILIES OF THE RICH WHITE POLITICIANS. IT'LL BE THE IMPOVERISHED PEOPLE -- ALL OUR **BLACK** AND **LATINO** BROTHERS AND SISTERS IN THE MILITARY, THAT'S WHO.

>SIGH< I'VE SEEN THIS ALL BEFORE. IT'S REALLY ABOUT THE **JEWS** -- THE ARABS HATE US... AND THEY HATE AMERICA, BECAUSE WE SUPPORT ISRAEL! WHY WON'T THEY LEAVE US ALONE ALREADY?

?

WHAT ARE WE SUPPOSED TO DO -- WAIT AROUND FOR ANOTHER 9/11? I SAY LET'S GO GET 'EM BEFORE THEY GET US. I MEAN, COME ON, THIS GUY IS **EVIL**. HE'S LIKE **HITLER** -- WHAT IF WE COULD'VE STOPPED HIM BEFORE HE KILLED TWELVE MILLION PEOPLE?!

I'M REALLY SCARED. IF WE DO THIS, WHAT WILL THE REPERCUSSIONS BE? WILL WE HAVE MADE THINGS **BETTER**, OR WILL WE HAVE MADE THINGS **WORSE**?

© 2002 HANSON + NEUWIRTH

CHELSEABOYS.COM

CHELSEA BOYS

BY GLEN HANSON and ALLAN NEUWIRTH

...SO I SAID TO MISS THING, "LOOK, HONEY"--

WHAT?!!

THE PINK TRIANGLE BOOKSHOP IS OUT OF BUSINESS? WHEN DID THIS HAPPEN???

I DUNNO.

WHAT DIFF'RENCE DOES IT MAKE? IT WAS JUST A BOOKSTORE, BABY. DIDN'T EVEN HAVE A BACKROOM!

ARE YOU KIDDING--?!

PINK TRIANGLE WAS PRACTICALLY A MONUMENT TO THE WHOLE GAY RIGHTS MOVEMENT...BESIDES, YOU HAVE NO IDEA WHAT THIS PLACE MEANS TO ME...

I REMEMBER COMING HERE WHEN I WAS 16 ON THE TRAIN FROM LONG ISLAND. GOD, I WAS SO SCARED THAT SOMEONE WOULD SEE ME-- BUT THIS WAS THE ONLY PLACE I COULD FIND BOOKS ABOUT WHAT IT MEANT TO BE GAY.

AND BELIEVE IT OR NOT, THIS IS WHERE I MET MY LOVER, PAUL, TWELVE YEARS LATER... I WAS PERUSING JOHN RECHY AND LARRY KRAMER--AND HE WAS PERUSING ME! ≥CHUCKLE≥

FOR YEARS, MY FRIENDS AND I USED THIS PLACE AS A MEETING PLACE ON PRIDE DAY. I CAN'T BELIEVE IT'S CLOSED. I GUESS I JUST TOOK IT FOR GRANTED IT WOULD ALWAYS BE AROUND...

BUT, DUDE, YOU CAN STILL GET GAY BOOKS ON THE WEB-- OR AT BARNES & NOBLE.

PLEASE. ONE LITTLE RACK IN BARNES & NOBLE CAN'T COMPARE WITH A WHOLE BOOKSTORE.

EVERY TIME ONE OF THESE GAY SHOPS DISAPPEARS, WE LOSE A PIECE OF OUR HISTORY. I'M AFRAID THAT SOME DAY NO ONE WILL EVEN REMEMBER IT WAS HERE!

HUH, I SEE WHAT YOU MEAN.

WELL, AH STILL SAY THIS WOULD'NA HAPPENED IF THEY'D HAD A BACK ROOM...

NO SERIOUSLY, I'M FEELIN' YA, BABY.

≥SIGH≥ C'MON. LET'S GO HOME.

© 2003 HANSON + NEUWIRTH

CHELSEABOYS.COM

ABOUT THE CARTOONISTS

Glen Hanson, a native of Toronto, is an internationally acclaimed designer, illustrator, writer, and art director. He has illustrated for clients such as *Entertainment Weekly, Newsweek, Variety,* Random House, VH-1, *Vogue, The New York Times, Maxim*, McDonald's, Grand Marnier, *British Vogue, GQ,* and *Esquire*. He also illustrated a cover for Blink-182's album *The Enema Strikes Back*, which won an AIGA award. Glen's G-man beefcake images are available as cards and other merchandise around the world, and his character designs have been seen on animated shows such as *Beetlejuice* and *Daria*. In 2000, Glen was nominated for an Annie Award for his art direction on MTV's *Spy Groove*.

Allan Neuwirth, a native New Yorker, writes, produces, directs, and designs for a wide variety of media, with a strong emphasis on comedy and animation. Some of his recent projects include producing/head writing *Fix and Foxi*, an animated series for European TV, Sesame Workshop's *Big Bag* for Cartoon Network, Jim Henson Productions' *Wubbulous World of Dr. Seuss* (for which he received a Writers Guild Award nomination), and the award-winning claymation series *Koki*. His host of cartoon writing credits includes *Courage the Cowardly Dog, Gadget and the Gadgetinis*, and *Dragon Tales*. Allan's first book, *Makin' Toons*, was published by Allworth Press in summer 2003.

Together, Glen and Allan have written stories for DC Comics' Cartoon Network comic books, collaborated on the graphic novel *Wonder Woman vs. The Red Menace* for DC's RealWorld line, and are creating several new animated TV series. For more information visit www.chelseaboys.com.